SMOLDERING

poems of desire

Avery Cassell

Pony Paws Press - 2025

Smoldering: poems of desire

Pony Paws Press
Greenfield, MA 01301 USA
stoicpress.bigcartel.com
averystoicpress@gmail.com

Smoldering: poems of desire/Avery Cassell
ISBN: 979-8-9887469-5-9

Cover designed by Avery Cassell
Cover: The Future Unveiled by Suzanne Valadon
(1912)

Pony Paws Press

Dedication

Smoldering: poems of desire is dedicated to
the painter Suzanne Valadon.

TABLE OF CONTENTS

A Handful of Prickly Threads

A thread of insincerity floats to the ground
a soft blue sparkling thirty inches of mohair
a cat toy or a half a fringe or something else
stretched from door jamb to door jamb
iron tacks holding it taut – and I trip
getting my ankles tangled up in starlight and night
my knees stained blue and silver from kneeling at
your boots
palms flat on the rug
I look up to see you rise
your body scrolling up from that length of lies
tendons and bones slipping through each filament
weaving together to form a wisp of a ghost
plaiting to create a you I hardly recognize.

I trip and I fall again and again and again
how many times can I bruise my knees on you
stuffing a skein of blue mohair into my mouth
your disingenuousness, a handful of prickly
threads
drool dribbling down the sides of my lips
knocking my head against your phantom boot.

There is something about this that I love
is it the abject position or the secrets?
a pushing into some dangerous country of the
heart?
I am comforted by how we excavate our thoughts
each sentence containing
gullies of truth and deceit
and yet you rise
to find me beneath you
I lay on the harsh wool carpet
exhausted, my cheeks tear-stained
disregarding your lies – to invite you in
now.

It's like I came 10,000 times
but it wasn't until you slapped me
that I was done.

A Burst of Red Seeds

There are ways of eating pomegranates
in Persia we prepare the fruit by pressing into it
with our thumbs
turning the fruit until we've softened
it, each seed cracking inside
then we bite the flesh to release the juices
as the sweetness gushes
sliding down our throats
staining our lips.

With my lips on your not quite a clit
not quite a cock
your special swell of flesh
your knob of a red berry
I suck.

Holding you down
my palms flat upon your thighs
pressed down hard
I can't help myself
and I growling nip your labia
my teeth white and sharp
each bite causing your wings
to engorge all hot and ripe

you yell with pleasure
I feel my cunt tightening and pounding.

We burst at once
our red, glistening seeds open
our hearts open
juices of our fruit
streaming sticky sweet
we shine.

Payment

And what of it?
a nick in the opening and I'm in.

A sliver of fingernail
a chink of metal
one hair.

We had clues
but paid no attention
as if there could ever be payment
for the past.

A drift of dust
a whiff of air
a bird wing sheltering
I close one eye
and am buried beneath you.

Morning Fruit

You peel me in the morning
a salty fruit of our invention
bisecting me with your grubby fingers
smelling of cheap, musty soap and bootblack.

I'm the half-dressed one
in Kelly green Jockey shorts
and a white shirt
on the edge of the bed, picking out my tie
and you, in grey wool dress pants and a blue shirt
the shirt that I embroidered
"morning head" on the cuff
straightening your tie while looking at me
I am sprouting sweet and wet and salt and hard
under your gaze.

We're getting ready to go to shul
on a Saturday morning
you see me hesitate
over the black tie with the blue chickens
my hand pink and clean
nails trimmed short
my thumb ring gleaming
and age spots a tawny brown

I touch the black silks lightly
choosing my necktie.

Your fingers move forward
reaching for my fly
pulling the knit fabric
to one side like a curtain
wrangling in
I am open and waiting
ties dropped to the floor and forgotten
thighs spread like jam on toast
sticky and you find your way in
I am the salty fruit you peel open
your fingers, the sweetest knife.

In the Playground, 9pm

To Dylan with mountains of affection

We walked past Delores Park at 9pm
the air all thick with loamy dampness
dirt and grass and the smell of the sea
the end of fall and start of winter
making the night feel longer.

It was unusually warm
warm enough for us to
tuck our hats into our pockets
take our jackets off
we were hand-in-hand for the first time
both of our palms sweaty
our hands the exact same size
fingers clasped together tightly.

After getting ice-cream
we walked up the palm tree lined sidewalk
to the playground
the night dark and sweet
our lips sticky with popsicles
the moon shining
high and white.

I ran up the longest slide,
gathering momentum
at the top, not seeing it
I slammed my forehead
into the metal safety bar
and looked around stunned
feeling my skin tender and a knot rising already
then I slid down giggling.

You got stuck in the rubber swing
swaying upside down
your shorts caught in the side chain
almost leaving you pantless
naked from the waist down
I unhooked you from the swing in the dark
we couldn't stop laughing.

I wonder –
if this had been a dream
like the kind about flying
or getting lost or funny monsters
the symbolism would have been blinding
I don't have an answer
but sometimes life feels like finding omens
there is meaning in tiny things

swings and slides
a knock on the head
leads to a loss of pants
let's run up that slippery slope of desire
our clothing falling by the wayside
into the velvety night.

Lupins on Twin Peaks

At the trolley stop looking left
fog drift
I know that if I see Twin Peaks
I'm facing away from the ocean
the Bay starts in a watch tower
a bed of seals
Market Street unwinding towards the Castro
then two hills rising
a winding narrow pathways
to the top of the right breast
where we fucked.

We visited Twin Peaks
the first day of the eleventh son
no, I meant the first day of the ninth visit
took the bus to the edge or pinocle
scrambling to some dusty rock
surrounded by scrubby California bushes
and lupins, tall and violet
and leaning back facing the Bay
leaning against a boulder
my overalls dropped to the ground
you curled your hand inside of me
the air smelled of the ocean, lupins, and come.

Never Calling

I'm an orphan
stroking my mustache
the prickly hairs, barely there
and you so far away
never calling
my fingertip on my upper lip
distracting me from wanting you.

My words are nothing
my thoughts nothing
my hand between my thighs
remembering the twist of your wrist
as your hand reaches in
and that shout of….that growl of
riding your arm and your hand like a train
bruising your wrist as I fuck you.

It's a simple nothing
the smallest ellipse of wonderment
and you so far away
never calling.

I'll tear out my cunt
from its roots
mail it to you
posting it with a million stamps
priority postage
sodden with unshed orgasms and tears
and you never calling
cavalier.

Written on My Thighs

Sunday night is a kick in the ass
swift expulsion from dreamland to servitude
a reminder that if I want a silk necktie
amber soap, goat cheese quiche
I need to trade my life for money
there, I said it
give up time over and over
like a starling flying into glass.

Sunday night is a single bed
of rusty nails or concrete
a letter that is never delivered
so you wonder if someone wrote
"I love you", but you'll never know
and after a while it doesn't matter
you fly into the glass then fall to the sidewalk
stunned, finally realizing you're trapped.

Sunday is listening to Nina Simone sing
your body sweaty and exhausted
tonight, I wonder if anyone will ever again
dip their fingers into me
to write "I love you" in fire
on my thighs.

Photo of my Mother at the Cabin, 1964

A photo of my mother
it's always a photo of someone's mother
and every photo with creased edges
she is the delicate angel of everyone's desire
the sand, the beach chair, the waves of water
all lapping towards her
three men in striped beach chairs
gravity works sideways – and their eyes
white v-neck t-shirts
or are they crew neck does it matter
cans of Carlsberg beer
clenched in sweaty palms
cigarettes and pipes.

Their eyes like antenna bobbing towards her
always her
my mother smiles for the camera and says "fuck
you"
her ruched swimsuit says "fuck you"
her lips say "fuck you"
her blue eyes – so cornflower blue
say "fuck you."

Maybe I'm imagining
her anger, her distance
because she was so Southern polite
each "fuck you" draped with flirtation
eyes icy.

The middle man is my father
he leers towards my mother
his friend to the left
leers towards my father and his wife
the man on the right
leers inwards, drool covering his balls
the camera man
leers towards all four
and I, a child of 11
I watch.

Washing Carla's Back by Candlelight

Carla is bathing at night, 1am
we're high, she and I
her back curved as I wash it
a pale freckled cliff
water running down in dribbles
over her shoulder blades in rivers
rivulets of soapy water
along her spine.

I kneel on green linoleum tiles
peeling beneath my knees
her head lowered and drooping
hair drifting
long strands floating
on the bath's surface.

I use a washcloth to clean her
not daring to touch her
breathless at her beauty
skin-on-skin
just my thumbs escaping
as I rub her broad back
from her waist to neck

I plow through soap bubbles
sliding over each tan mole
the whorls of my thumbprints
burning into her skin
the furrow of her spine
hills of muscle flanking each vertebra
her wet smooth flesh
yielding under my hand
under the washrag.

The window cracked open
the bare bulb overhead
turned off
incense smokey in whirls
three sputtering candles
set upon the toilet seat
flames wavering in the draft
candlelight bathing the room
in gold, the moon in midnight
we are illuminated.

Your Ass a Snowy Field

How was I to know?
the curve of your waist
and then your ass as wide
as a snowy field
I tramp along
my hands gripping the edges of you
rubbing my labia over your boots
tall black boots and nothing else
I press harder and slide
my bruised cunt strains
to grasp the leather.

Oh, your ass
I inhale your smell
the creases of inside
dank and dark
the smell of you
a rough sweating sex of your ass
I want to sink into you
clinging to your waist
reaching around for your right nipple
as I fuck you.

All it Takes is One Airline Ticket

There is a color inside me
yellow barbed in my chest
fire and bright
blooming explosions as we touch
fingers meeting across the miles.

It's hard to connect with you
I want to melt my yellow
like a spilling yolk
English nurseries and nannies
crops, fireplaces and egg cups
yellow all warm and sticky
down our sides
I mean our thighs.

My cunt aches with wanting
painful – all pinching and restless
desire a golden lightning bolt
running through my body
and I know this;
all it takes is one airline ticket
for the pinch to become warm and sticky
running down my thighs.

***After Seeing Sick: The Life and Death of
Bob Flanagan, Supermasochist Together***

What am I waiting for?
a you and another you
birds fly past, swooping into the night air
I want to be them
flying away from you.

You hold me
we talk and we talk
about everything
you hold me
and we talk
and we talk curiously about each other.

Nothing is bad
the sound of your thoughts
the heat of your body
stay with me all night
after you leave
one foot on the windowsill
the other on a treetop
you fly away.

You say you love me wholly now
I know that
remembering
I've decades of whole love
from people that stopped short.

I feel a full-stop in your good-bye
it may be my imagination
or maybe my impatience
I look at the swooping birds
wishing to escape
the knowledge of limitations.

You left a plum
on my windowsill
it fell out of your pocket
tumbling with a soft plop
a gift
or maybe a fortune
is this unripe desire?
you've told me that's inside of you
softening and ripening
just wait
patience.

So I wait to hold you
wait for your heart to flutter open
and long for wings
when I desire too much.

Growly Bear

I come flying in
arms stretched out and reaching
fingers stretched out
never finding my destination
reaching for the you I don't want
anymore.

I don't want you flying with me
I don't want shiny things
sparkling in the sky
like iridescent bug wings
clouds drifting across mountaintops
a bed of fluff and tears
only props to distract me.

Go away
let growly bear
grab you with their paw
tear you apart
scatter you to the trees
until you're impaled upon branches
the fruit of heartbreak
while I float in the overcast sky of my heart

I can't think through
this spasm of fuck and shared bread
that I'm left with.

I'm naked now
enveloped in the mist
my hands upon my accordion
legs splayed and leaning sadly
listing left until my cheek rests
upon a hillside
watering the orchards with my tears
each note is different – I see that now
cut these ropes so I can fly away.

I'm friends with growly bear
she lives in the fronds of curled leaves
ferns on the forest floor
waiting for me to toss her a treat
and flying through my tears, I do.

Princes and Kings

For B, who wanted to be a boy from the start

I imagine you
ten years old and laying in your bed
on a single mattress with white cotton sheets
the breeze blows the window's curtain open
letting in the cool night air, smelling of ozone.

You take one small fingertip
your skin bathed, new and soft
smelling of Ivory soap and clean fingernails
touch your jaw, pressing in to discover the
structure of your body
your face, the muscles, the epidermis, the blood,
the pores
you touch, wishing to find hair, sprouts whirling
to the surface
the smallest beard resting on your chin like a
crown.

You are a prince
you have traveled distances
and now you rest between, always between
36 years later, you stroke your chin
eking out the differences between child and adult.

26

I'll hunt a pelt for you
take your dream and cover you with it tenderly
smoothing, caressing your warm flesh
wanting so much.

You'll find it between day and night
between fragments of time
jumbled until linearity is unimportant
the ozone of thunderclap and change
lifting you, a growling bear
face raised and hair bristling
your beard growing, growing.

You laying in your bed
me, touching your jaw with my bathed fingertip
the graying crown
we are the kings we dreamed of.

.

Lili Marlene Gets Fucked

Confined to barracks – no longer in the street
strapped to a red wooden kitchen chair
splinters poking and pricking her hands
pale thighs splayed and freckles dancing
her German ankles tied to a rung
bound tightly and eight legs rest on the cold floor
the officer's, the chair's, and Lili Marlene's.

Lili tosses her head
hair swishing
she will not break
for she is Lili Marlene.

Lili of the lamplight, that shines upon her face
far from the dark corners of the room
cobalt shadows between her open legs
soft legs a shining golden light
the officer touches tiny on her thighs
fingers crawl goose-stepping
up towards Lili's cunt
Lili Marlene stretches for more
stretches for the officer's hand
the lantern softly gleams upon on each caress
the blunt hand and soft cunt coming together

parted lips to kiss good-night
each of the officer's fingers
the red chair tipping precariously
as Lili's cunt holds the officer's hand
holds it close.

Lili asks,
"is this love, or is it a flower pressed to my heart?"
opening from her heart
the stamen piercing her throat as she cries out
the officer's teeth are sharp
as they devour her from the legs down
then up again on Lili's body towards her neck
leaving a road of small wounds
bruises marching from her shins to her clavicle
each bruise a kiss, a blooming over her breast
Lili sighs with desire;
and my love for you renews my might
for you, Lili Marlene.

November Full Moon

Tonight, the full moon is my lover
traveling with me from the bus to my home
a tangle of silvery light
winding its way like cigarette smoke
shining around my body.

Moon rays float down
wrap my arms and cheeks
white lace, white ribbons
a wispy coolness
holding me with her radiance.

Vanilla

8am on a Sunday morning
we walk to Orphan Andy's for eggs and toast
down Market Street
the night still clinging to us
the violet wash of dawn
shimmers over the dirty sidewalk
we're careful not to step in unintended
consequences
watching our words
as they murmur from our lips like steam.

Once in the diner
we order from the waiter in the kilt
with a studded belt spelling "naked"
everything makes me think of your ass
so I gulp coffee and change the subject.

Your ass is my unintended consequence
and I mince through this swamp of desire carefully
like one of those queens from around the corner
lifting my sequined skirt to avoid any mess
it's no use – my words are frippery
unimaginable
and each sentence is a nothing;

blithe and meaningless
I could say anything
like "butter from rare cows living two miles from
Stonehenge"
my words are air.

Eating our toast nibbly – quickly
we prepare to leave Orphan Andy's
get the check from the kilted waiter
rushing forward and home
the yellow sun rising over our bed
like a schmaltzy greeting card
illustrating socialism with women
bending over crops in the fields
or maybe just crops, and I bend over
my ass and your ass and unintended consequences
flying like birds
I bend over.

After four days of being sequestered
fucking, nibbling on chocolate
we get dressed and visit a friend
for tea and company
once there, all I can do is querulously ask
from the floor at Dylan's
as I kneel at your feet

cleaning my dried come off of your
new brown leather pants with my tongue
"why so vanilla?"
you both laugh at me.

You chuck me under my chinny-chin-chin
and ask me, "What part was vanilla?
the part where I stuffed two feet of chain up your
cunt?
or the bit where you were tied up
with a steel egg in your ass and I was fisting you?
maybe it was where we were wearing boots, strap-
ons and nothing else,
and you were sucking my cock?
or was it when I was beating you with a baseball
bat?
or was it here and now, with you licking my pants?
tell me little Bird."

The truth is this;
the vanilla is the soft bits
which terrify me, leads me to whine
it's all the tender parts;
the part where we lay together
nuzzling like orphan ponies
the part where we wrap ourselves

around each other like seaweed
drowning in our bed of kisses and come
not getting up until 3 in the afternoon
and then only to bring back
giant bowls of heated up stew
eating under the worn-out quilt
the cat back on the bed for this interlude.

The parts where we sleep together
kissing each other even through our snores
shoulders, legs, backs, necks
all warm flesh belonging to one another and loved
the rich vanilla of desire
rolling through our mouths like holiday candy
and I want you again and again.

Making Curry

There's steam in the kitchen
humid puffs, fragrant
you stir the curry
spices and onion frying in oil
your wooden spoon slicing through the coconut
milk
dipping in and sideways making small waves
your hand bent slightly at the wrist
your index finger extended
I am mesmerized, distracted by this motion
your finger - your hand.

I quarter a sweet potato
peeling it first
because I want to feel the skin curl off tenderly
falling in orange and brown curls
hold the potato and slice
accidentally slip the knife into my skin
opening a cut on my right finger
suddenly seeping blood
I bring my finger to my mouth and suck
you look up from the curry
watching me now - intent.

The waves have caught up with me
I smear blood over my lips while glancing up
head lowered slightly
cutting my eyes at you
looking up like I'm on my knees
and you're in my mouth
I taste the steam of curry and blood
rolling over my tongue
you lay the spoon down to hold my hand
my finger passing through your lips
inside your mouth
your tongue soft and wet
across my cut – intent
with desire.

Pandemonium

Am I inconsolable or incomprehensible
with your fingers inside of me
curled like a bird claw, something flying
and I on the edge of the bed
the edge of the falling sky
holding my breath inside
and then letting go with clamor of noise
flapping wings fluttering from my mouth
a pandemonium of need.

A puffery of noise flying over the wires at night
miles away across mountains and water
and you tell me that it will be weeks
90 days before you are here again
my heart is a nothing, voided
a bird skeleton with no organs inside
and I listen for you slicing through
the air like starlight
our mouths open to one another.

Buttercup

Early morning, I'm half asleep
my ass curled towards your belly
three blankets
warm and heavy over us
shelter.

Your two fingers on my asshole
spreading spit then lube
like spreading jam
sweet in circles inwards
I rub back against you – more.

Your sticky fingers reach around
my sleepy body toasty
pull my nipples and twist
my ass levitates
your dick pushing forward and back
forward and back
my asshole opening up like a buttercup
soft petals falling away to reveal the stamen
hold this under your chin to see if you like butter
and I do
all slippery inside.

At the same moment
like choreographed ice-skaters
graceful gold glitter twirling
we meet, you inside me and I around you
eight inches of silicone and lube
waking up dreams
slick sweat
my back to your chest holding one another
your mouth, your words covering me so sticky.

Woolen blanket fort
holding our groans as we fuck
my cunt and ass tightening
my dick hard
your hands holding my tits like reins
your hips and my ass are pistons
something mechanical
chugging along
where one can't move without the other
your teeth on my shoulder
all drool and sharp – you bite
everything wet, buttercup.

Displacement of Skin

A bird or bug
something flying in the air
lands on my rounded shoulder
its wings a whisper
that sends me spinning
a gift from you.

I unwrap this present
you touch me and I feel spools of
yellow and periwinkle blossoming inside
my organs are gone
all I have is sex
displacement of what?

Is skin the organ that holds sex in place
or is it sex itself?
flesh is more than skin
the flesh of my shoulders is a bruise
which moves as I walk and talk
which shifts like an earthscape
reminding me sharply of your touch.

The flesh of my upper chest
is boutonnièred with your tooth prints
my wrists are circled in blue and violet
is flesh the reminder
or is it the slow molasses feeling of coming
as it slides from my cunt to my throat
down my legs when I remember
your hands and looking at you?

I wash my flesh each morning
steaming water, scented soap
scrubbing dreams from my skin
so that memories
have a place to nest.

My Imaginary Girlfriend I

We sat across from one another at 9am
sated from a 7am booty call
is it a booty call if you wake up spooned together
like bark on a tree
layer upon layer of time and love.

We ate peppered bacon and omelets
then I left to buy fabric for our picnic quilt
while you stayed home
to refinish an Eastlake rocker
the wind blew me to Berkeley
the wind blew clean air into our apartment
fumes rising and James Brown bellowing
that it's a man's world.

When I returned with three yards of Indian Ikat
unfurling it to show you
all our future deviled eggs and iced tea
appeared in its length
sleeping in a secret meadow
the scent of grass and redwoods
unfurling our memories
we admired the slate blue, dirt brown, orange rust
the cat demanded food
and we retired for a Sunday afternoon nap.

My Imaginary Girlfriend II

My imaginary girlfriend
has cold feet
literally, not figuratively
she rubs her toes and heels
against my calves to keep warm
I'm hot for her.

My imaginary girlfriend
snores every night
she doesn't notice the soft rumble
of her breath
because she's asleep.

My imaginary girlfriend
can't resist me in the morning
she turns on her side
holding me closer
like I'm her blanket
our skin pressed tightly together.

My imaginary girlfriend
straddles my soft hips
like her favorite pony
I neigh and wiggle
cows abound.

My Imaginary Girlfriend III

My imaginary girlfriend hears
thunder in the distance
and moves from
the sofa to close the windows
softly.

Our rescue cat in the kitchen
eating shrimpies
her tail a white plumed boa
the tip waving
slowly.

My imaginary girlfriend
pours salted cashews
into a green
leaf-shaped dish
brings it to me
quietly.

Her feet warm
in woolen socks
keeping each piggie
toasty, she snuggles
next to me

sleepily.

I'm soft
slowly watching
quietly
sleepily
thunder and lightning
tucking us into bed.

My Imaginary Girlfriend IV

My imaginary girlfriend is warm
and I say this as the furnace turns on
inadvertently.

That is to say,
the setting was 55°
and it was under 55° in the living rooms
causing the heat to blast in reaction.

I have one cat on my shins
another sprawled across my thighs
hoodie plus hat plus fingerless gloves
in addition to cats
it's not enough.

My imaginary girlfriend
scoots over on the sofa
making room for me
I snuggle my nose against her neck
she smells like snow and hot tea
flannel sheets and whispers
the cats purr.

My Imaginary Girlfriend V

My imaginary girlfriend has snow boots
she slips them in to run out back
knobbly knit scarf trailing
a woolen tail that I follow
we make snowballs and throw them
lopsided, with minimal accuracy
twirling like teenage squirrels
slipping, the cold snow nearly to our boot tops
I chase her
cornering her between the peeling side of the
house
and the dark towering cedar trees
snow plows rattling past
flakes falling thick and sticky
I grab her by the scarf
pull her close and kiss her icy lips warm.

Jealousy
For Dina, with all my love

One baby is discarded like zwieback
drool conferring on either end
the center the driest confection
suitable for teething
that spurt of growth
from fat red cheeks
to something more temperate
a practice baby
the naked one without, embellishment.

The other baby is embraced
like a dimpled baby's bottom
or chubby arms and legs
lifting and lifting
(lifting cow)
baby number two gets it all
walks in the park
their head shoved down the toilet
until they can't stop squealing with delight
toys and tutus and jewels
until they can't stand up
the donkey can't stand up any more
what's the ugliest part of your body?

lifting cow over and over and over.

Baby number one watches
astounded
their baby love bitter crumbling
scattered in the park
for the sparrows
to feast upon at night.

Cruising with my Gay Boyfriend
For Tony

Sitting on a rainy Sunday afternoon
at the queer coffee shop
in front of the plate glass window
with a clear view of the café
and the wet sidewalk
across from one another, grinning
the tabletop collaged with vintage
newspaper clippings
our mismatched coffee cups resting
on "Pride float – 1983" and "Queen Victoria –
1987" respectively.

We cruise guys in the cafe
as they sidle towards the restroom door
casting eyes sideways
gazing at round asses and half-mast bulges
crooked smiles and broad shoulders
until they find a trick
hang out in the cramped foyer
read the bulletin board incessantly
loiter for one another
the smell of lust, sugar, and coffee fills the air
sweet and moist from the rain.

I feel your foot rub mine
a tapping and slouch as you touch my leg
a long firm stroke
you smile slyly at me
reach under the table for my hand
hidden from the gay boy's eyes
the neon café sign flashes rainbow lights upon us
violet, blue, red, yellow lights mottled by the rain
our hands held tight with infatuation
far from all your ex-tricks and tricks-to-be's eyes.

I'm your first girlfriend
we're unsteady with this unexpected
this unexpected everything
"I love your face when you come" you whisper
and I turn pink from my cheeks to my ears
my blush of rushing blood
starting in my face and running down
my neck, shoulders, breasts, belly,
cunt, thighs and to my toes

the rainbow light glowing over us
showering us with joy
our hands secretly entwined
as we look at the boys
wonder who likes it rough

who likes it soft as a sun shower
who murmurs like falling snow
who likes to be on their knees
who you had done
who you want to do and how
finish our coffee
disentangle each hand and foot
from under the table
to walk home in the rain.

Courting

The girls in Western Massachusetts
court you with raspberry bushes
spiky shrubs that fruit later on
romance tinted with mulch and roots
"I have extra" they whisper
a wink and a sly glance.

The raspberry produces fruit quickly
watered with kisses and moonlit tangles
sweat and sighs
you tease my flesh with berries
squishing each berry with your calloused fingertips
before placing it on my tongue.

The Synchronized Queer Swim Team

In this town all the fortune cookies
end with "with a queer".

You left to go back to Seattle this morning
your boots and gamba by the doorstep
a pile of hats like a stacked Melton cake
backpacks and suitcases in disarray
I miss you already.

I find your black checked scarf on the coat-hook
a blue wool shirt folded
on the dining chair ready to be mended
your metal water bottle on the kitchen counter
next to a box of breakfast tea
your new bus pass on the dresser
next to my IMsL pass
reminders in each room.

We're swimming underwater
to Martha and the Muffins
the Synchronized Queer Swim Team
cigars floating above the waves
smoke twirling hand-in-hand
into the night fog

my long thin legs
intertwining
with your thick hairy legs
we float like curling
unfurling seaweed in warm waters.

Fortune cookies keep us fed
crumbs floating like tiny canoes on the waves
our fortunes surrounding us;
you will be happy -- with a queer
a business proposition will end well -- with a queer
your loyalties are clear with friends -- with a queer
an unexpected event will soon make your life
more exciting -- with a queer
the stars shine like oysters -- with a queer.

The Bittersweet Pink Full Moon

I lay naked in spring
arms and legs spread wide
inviting the season
to overcome me.

A crabapple tree dropping petals
a pillow of pale pink petals
billowing, billowing in the night
the pink full moon glowing
as I tumble and tunnel
blossoms sticking to my bottom
beneath my breasts
in the folds behind my knees
pink petals stick to my armpits
nearly smothering me.

The bloom's spicy perfume
burrowing into my heart
I'm rollicking in the fragrance
twisting and abandoned
of bittersweet memories
of you.

Lucille was a Snake-Handler
For David

Somewhere between asking me if I came
and what my boundaries were
you told me your mother was a snake-handler
not some quaint traveling woman
with a floral woolen shawl
like you'd see on a circus poster
but more like a Minoan snake goddess
from the wet Appalachian hills of West Virginia.

Her name was Lucille
and she was a Pentecostal
only five foot two, with long red hair
and a flair for seeking out the devil
which she found in you, her son
the devil encased in fire
floating over your body like a caul.

She fucked you for one decade – ten years
before you reared back upon
your boyish cloven-hooves
eyes flashing and fingers
balled into a small, damp fist
to punch her straight away
on her holy freckled nose

blood gushing
as you to flee from the snake-filled hills
and into my bed
Lucille was a snake-handler.

1am in San Francisco

Laying in my bed with you at 1am
sheets tangled
our breasts mashed together
your breath moist upon my shoulder
listening to Nico whisper "Sunday Morning"
waiting for sleep
with its tender dreams
this is all I ever wanted.

It's a cool San Francisco night
filled with fog and promise
your small hand pressed
flat on my belly
curved around me in love
you hand hold me
welded together
your pink palm to my soft skin.

My leg thrown over your thigh
the outer edge of my leg rests
against your cunt
your clit hard
your sweetness damp
spreads like rays of moonlight

your taste travels through my blood vessels
from my leg to my tongue
my lips part in need to hold
your cunt in my mouth
my mouth a cave for your cunt to dwell
inside steaming.

Oh, it is that quiet night
moment of us
I want to lay sweaty
breathe our smell into my heart
come coating my bones
spicy and dark
filled with you forever.

Sweet Boy

Face down on the bed
I'm the boy of our dreams
every word is inadequate
I say we fucked so violently
that I bruised the top of my head
so what, so what.

I mean to say
the words "sweet boy"
whistled through the air
two syllables swirling thickly
until they landed on my shoulder
rushed through me
a cloud of locusts or bees
a thick storm of a buzz
each wing beating.

And I lay there with your voice
in the pit of my cunt, in my ass
drooling damp on the pillow
slamming my head
into the wooden headboard.

What are we doing?
I stand weak and flushed
sometimes I want to add
all the words, the syllables together
form sentences that stretch the distance
from your mouth to mine and back
I cannot talk about
this swarm growing between us
a hedge of greenery
a living thing in the springtime
we rush in eyes half-closed
with coded messages
sometimes a cigar is just a smoke.

Baby Love at Age 13
For Patty

It's raining this morning
flannel sheets remind me
of being 15 and in love
although at 15, I was not in love
and had never slept between flannel sheets.

How can morning rain
remind me of a nonexistent memory?

I remember you and I at 13
girlish, but not girly
sleepovers and kisses
my mother making us buckwheat pancakes
on Sunday morning
the snow piling up in the alley behind my house
white iridescent flakes
falling under the yellow streetlight
"Baby Love" playing on my transistor radio
as our legs tangled together
under the wool blanket
your hands smoothing my skin
we were so soft and young.

This never happened
not with you
it was another girl
we lived in different countries
you're 10 years younger
you hate Motown
and today, it's raining
you're 3,000 miles away
I'm drinking hot sugary tea
willing this memory of you
into existence.

Walking on Coals

Fucking you is like walking on coals
I move forward, feet tender
and I, tenacious
your hand inside of me
a slap to my chest and I open up.

My heart is in a cave
the cave deep and dark
my heart a red pounding spot
revealed, as you come crashing through.

I open my mouth, my cunt, my palm
and the past roars out
dying lovers, final fucks, and tears
shine from my body
beacons.

There's too much for me
these stories are a light
they blind me and I flinch
I turn my head, my heart, my hand
they illuminate you
the now and the past.

A slap to my chest
and I am cleansed
of the cloud of grief
that lives in the red spot of my heart
placing each foot flat on these coals
we fuck.

Slip-On Hornet

You said "slip-ons"
and my heart stopped.

Who knew that word
would cause a rush of heat
not me.

I'd never heard the word before
"slip-ons"
I watched as each syllable dripped
from your lips
like honey.

I swear
you could have said "hornet's nest"
and I would have gasped
anticipating
the next word falling
from your mouth
opening my heart.

Eating Loss: a Tea Time Poem

How many times can I nibble
off the edges of my heart
like ginger candy
beef jerky or peach fruit leather
my teeth grinding into the night
a lullaby that ends sleep.

In dreams you're tying my ankles together
binding my wrists
one bone over the other
crisscross applesauce
my breath stopped
evaporating like cumulonimbus clouds
portending whirlwinds
of icy hail.

I chew slowly
lingering with the bitter taste of us
my heart the most tender of devices
beating the scent
of jasmine and tuberose
into the dark.

I spread my legs
mistaking my eager flesh's wet clenching
for escape
slowly I taste the loss of love
I swallow the past whole
letting it fill my throat, expanding
memories sealing my heart
shut
a gift that I eat.

The Last Time We Fucked
For Bunny

I measure everything by the distance
from the last time we fucked until now
the last time we fucked was after some party
I was there alone, or at least not with you
the room was full of feminists
listening to Holly Near
and talking earnestly about Reagan
so I got drunk on vodka and missed you.

They didn't want you there
and if you somehow were at that party
you would have snarled
that they were fucking classist bitches
just like that, all teeth and attitude
then you would have swept me out of there
getting us both banned for a while
or at least until they wanted to
score some 'ludes or some strange
which is what the straight boys called it
and that is what you were
with your derelict blue collar
bad girl anger.

70

I drank until I had to beg them
to take me to your apartment
me all blurred and needy and crying for you
you were crashing at some Army vet's
in a cheap duplex in the South End
you let me in and we stumbled
onto the blue polyester sleeping bag
it was on the living room floor
spread out in front of the big television
picture on and sound off.

I promised to take you away to New York city
where we could be free
I left you in the morning
five years later
you overdosed on the bathroom floor
of a Mexican fast food restaurant
your junkie girlfriend leaving you to die
she walked out
with a bag of cheap burritos
and no guilt.

I wailed walking in circles
in circles for the loss of you
you lying on the cool, greasy tile floor dying
and me sober living in a farmhouse.

Fuck this, fuck it all
I want to redo our last fuck and make it magic
spread out the sleeping bag in the starry night and
lay like clouds or colts
in the moonlight all blue and sweet
when we were magic
sometimes, we were.

Field of Cherries

A field of cherries,
red, round and sweet
mounds of loamy earth
fragrant with juice and twigs
something sugary and buried.

Laying on the dirt
sunlight washing over us
the thorny bushes nearby
cherry pits and bird bones
beneath our bottoms -
beneath our bottoms.

We ate until we had rashes
spots covering our white bellies
rounded, full of juice
under the ragged bushes
the smell of new spring
humid air surrounding us.

Rat skulls crunch under our hands
their tiny yellow teeth
curved into rodent anchors
snagging our palms

our blood surrounding the punctures
we suck each other's wounds
our lips red and sweet.

There is a field of cherries
waiting in my heart
fruit lying on the ground
one side plump and the other rotting
decaying into the earth
bursting open ripe
under the sky.

Twigs lay thickly in the paths
we push our way through
as if the bramble is water
clenching our cherries in our fists
sticky juice staining our knuckles
sliding over our hands, our thin fingers.

And here, a murky brook
moss-covered stones
we catch the rocks
agate and carnelian
cold and hard, smooth and fine
we store them inside one another
our cunts are slippery pockets.

The brook is a waterway
our bellies roll in ecstasy
as we lay down
curled on the muddy crick edge
cherries and rocks – bones and sticks
surrounding us as we lay hand-in-hand
your lips breathing dreams into my neck.

We are together
small animal skulls crackling
beneath us
the juice of the fruit dripping
down our thighs
hot whispered breath buried
between our breasts
the fresh dirt holding us
our bodies growing fields of cherries.

A Box of Heart

My heart has been boxed up like candy
something special that will make your teeth ache
a cold snowy shot —
one bite and you'll turn around
flying away on bird feathers
running on gazelle legs all spindly and fast.

Each year, a ribbon
winding through the night
weaving its way home
to a you I never knew that I missed.

Bite open my heart
tear it with your yellow teeth
hot breath ripping through muscle and pain
open me up with promises
loosen each year with your tongue
and swallow my sorrow.

Thoughts I Never Had

Sometimes my thoughts are oblique
they slither out of my mouth like river snakes
long green bodies tickling my lips
they're harmless, I suppose
with a sneaky grace.

Some snakes hibernate
staying in my cranium
curled up and seemingly sleeping
waiting to dance in my dreams
or to live in words written in invisible ink
letters written in a mirror.

Your words rise and fall,
your voice through the wires
your face and chest
an image on my monitor
your words rise and fall
like grape soda through a straw
the purple bubbles
foaming towards my mouth
my lips sucking you in
you say "hot" and now I'm wet.

I know what I want
my snakes are here in my open palm
you say "hot", and now I'm wet
I'm holding them out to you – a gift
they wave coolly to you
you're a snake-charmer in a fairy tale
or they are ocean foliage
it all comes back to water
you smile, open mouthed and tongue tip showing
your hands reaching out.

I swear there are no hidden snakes in my skull
plaited together scales overlapping
waiting to unravel their stories
dozing in the heat of my head – slumbering
and I believe myself
knowing that the unexpected is just a drop of
blood away
that this is how stories are written
in invisible ink and in a mirror
I believe myself
you say "hot" and now I'm wet.

The Physicality of Sleep

I want.

There's simplicity in the
smooth slip of cotton
along the length of my leg
my palm rubbing the fur
of my country squire belly
the buttery smell of burning cedar.

It's night
that perfect moment
wakening ends, sleeping begins
naked, long like taffy
loving the touch of my shoulder
my flesh downy and warm
my curved muscle.

The wet between my legs
as I stretch top to bottom
my cat purring swishy tailed
in the crock of my knees
my deflated down pillow cradling my head
just so.

And I want this minute
to last
I want sleep
with dreams
I want the salty smell of you
beside me.

What Fits There?

And well you ask
my bleating bird
my unwashed sparrow –
what fits there?

Your hand
a stone
a promise
a cold steel ball
words on paper.

I want it all
any and everything
feel the shape and volume
of what you place inside of me
my cunt is your nest
your cave, your home
the edges vibrate throughout my belly
cresting through my chest
an ocean of desire.

A Cloak of You

You're making wings on my back
the spread of the sound of the force so hard
and I can't think at all
all thoughts dispensed
dissipating, let loose.

I love my flesh as its molded by you
then the whole of you laying on me
spit first — so it's your mouth your belly
a cloak of you, a creature
long and sweaty
giving birth to bruises.

The gaze exchanged
when you hit me
we visit a shared country
a map to us
I look and I look
constantly, we look together.

Will your hand fit in my cunt?
will each tentacle finger wiggle?
you twist and torque
as you burrow into me

and I'm fucking you
I feel waves of ocean and periwinkle
inside of me.

The smell of you
I'm always sniffing my way
nose twitching, nostrils flaring
I'm a rat or a dog
needing to mesmerize my path home
your hair a tickling snort
your armpit desire settling into my throat
your cunt a wet
so hard I want to cry.

A long smooth cut
and I breathe it open
a star — it's light
polish me with blood
like a lucky penny.

I want to be bent over
like a sailor
and fucked.
is that too concise?
slow, then fast
and almost out – wait a second

then sliver in
motions so delicate
a souffle of fuck
fuck me into another galaxy.

And you are the ass of my dreams
with your spread of white skin
waiting – and yes I want you
tell me how big, how fast, how deep
suddenly I am nervous
a girl with worries
that I will be clumsy and awkward
when all I want is to
throw myself into you.

There are things I want
an airway of whooshing I cannot stop
the country of our skin
our kisses torrid
with jungle undergrowth
muggy and wet
the sliding of our bodies
over, that slippery
one into the other steaming
geography changes.

Your Shoulder so Velvet

The comfort of your shoulder
in the early morning
pressed to my lips
like a scrap of velvet
clenched between my sticky fingers.

I stroke your skin imagining
the blood shimmering beneath the surface
blonde hairs flecked
a meadow of goldenrods
erect and swaying in the spring breeze
your smell - sweet like 5am
wisps of dreams, porridge, and coffee
transport me skywards.

Your Bitey-ness to You

Teeth.
How else could anything about your bitey-ness
start
but with teeth
all sharp and ready to bite-bite me
my hand, my ass
and you do so love to bite.

The first time the yellow dog came
was to my attic bedroom
a small afterthought of a room
on a humid, Ohio summer night
with the cobalt blue bug zapper killing moths
right outside one of the tiny windows
the buzzing noise
and the soft plop of dead bugs
as they sizzled and floated down
the shine of the blue electric light
flowing into my bedroom cathedral.

Ted and I were inside fucking
Ted all big and growly
standing over me
like a giant sexy animal

all shoving it hard into my ass
and me face-down
over the side of the bed
my ass bare and arms splayed up
tossing my head from side to side
grunting, sweat gathering along my spine
the way I loved it
holding my wrists together
wanting to fuck the summer out of us both
fuck every capillary open
fuck ourselves senseless
or maybe overflowing with
the best kind of sense.

Just then, I heard a grrr
a prowling near my head
a shadow of something yellow
a passing furry
something
and I saw the dog
cadmium yellow with pointed teeth
and a grin
a lick over their teeth
spittle hanging down like a party favor
manifested by this glorious ass-fucking.

I followed the dog with my eyes
as they circled the bed
pacing around and around
they cackled with the joy of pleasure
looming close and leering
with needle teeth and lolling pink tongue
flapping in the humid air
incisors sharp and ready to bitey-bitey me
and me eager, wanting them
wanting them to gnaw on me
their truffle with a cream center
their treat of a bone.

Oh my growly dog
my precious terrible creature
my dog that only comes
when my blood boils up and over
I want you here this winter
growling, prowling around my bed
bite-biting me on my belly
sucking out my sweetness
until I become you
my darling dog
and you become me.

Breath

Sunday afternoon
I'm balanced mid-flight
wearing black riding boots
and nothing else
laughing back at you
head thrown back
one heel on the 9th stair
and the other on the 10th.

I can still feel each slap
my knees sore from
kneeling on the living room carpet
your hands holding me still
and hitting me
I'm seashell pink from your hand
there will be bruises
violet blooms on my ass.

You call me downstairs
and throw me to the floor again
I fall
grateful for the speed of your touch
as I hurl to the ground
I love the air against my skin

as I move so quickly
the rough of you
shoving me unexpected.

Then you sit astride me
denimed thighs on either side of my torso
pinning me
binding me immobile
your hand that holds my nostrils
shut so I cannot breathe
you smell comfortingly
of tobacco and cunt.

You lay your lips on mine – we kiss
you give me your used breath
the breath that has already
traveled throughout your body
swirls inside the cavern
formed by our joined mouths
our lungs bellow together
you breathe for me and into me
we glow inside one another
the air that's within us, sparkling
desire and love.

Not in Love

I'm not in love
writing mash notes to you
or anyone else
that caught my attention
a casualty of my childhood
and yearnings for a home.

The bunny fur soft of my cat
hot water scented
sliding over my belly
holding my shoulder
skin between the covers at night
a nighttime snack
three sweet raisins and a crumble of cheddar.

I imagine a you
inside of my heart and ass
sweet jasmine a clout of morning
transcendent blue sky
realer than pavement
my flesh hot and tender
as I skid into dreams.

The niblet of pleasure
sharp rodent teeth reminding me
of the bloodiness of life
without love or at least
without you.

Slick

I'm slick
I reach between my legs with two fingers
and inside, I'm so slick
like horse spit or snail trails
nothing like girls
no delicate doily.

I gather scoops of my come
on my two hooked fingers
bring them to my mouth — wet
to eat myself for breakfast.

You're in your bed
miles away imagining
my horse spit slickness
riding on your thigh
like a pony girl
neighing loudly.

I fuck myself with my fingers
pull my mane – my labia
then spread my wet
over my belly
braying for more.

Let Loose in Death

The moment of your death
slammed into an oak tree
slammed into a boulder
slammed into whatever
immoveable nearby object
that a beater car could drive into.

The driver was your husband
drunk and high
loose and lividly screaming at you
sloppy spittle and curses spilling out
cigarettes flying through the air
fast food bags crumpled
were you afraid
or was it just another drive home.

The moment of your death
I was 2,418 miles away
naked but for black boots and bruises
naked but for kisses and come
naked, sprawled face-down
a hand inside of my cunt
waves of come shooting out
drenching my boots
it was the first time like that for me.

The police said that you
took your time dying
your drunk husband watched
unable or unwilling to move
closer. Did he light another cigarette
your moans mixed with his smoke?
the landscape full of hard objects
the tree, the rock, the signpost
watching your dying
and you wrapped a bloody death
an animal at the end.

Was that moment of my coming
salty come pouring high pressure
the moment you died
both of us let loose
we who hold so tightly
onto our suffering.

The Roly-Poly of Surrender

You slipped your paw inside of me
like you were running to meet a bus
all full speed ahead
no hesitation.

Me – I rolled over
because that is what hedgehogs do best
roly-poly
I rolled over in a soft ball of surround
of surrender
of love.

It was night,
nightingales blooming,
jasmine chirping
the moon was in our bed
and stars shone from my cunt
as we roly-poly
joined together.

The Scent I'm Missing

The scent of your shoulder
the warm, mushroom dank smell
of you when we've been fucking
we're bears standing with claws extended
our bellies hanging like tufts of ermine
that soft fur
teeth big and yellow
our breath closer than a cloudbank
hanging over an airport.

I sniff for our smell
in your armpits and down your ribcage
I'm a rat trying to gnaw my way
into the cave of your heart
I snort lower, kissing your thigh
my lips soft on your skin
our smell wafting upwards
encircling us tightly.

I miss you already
it isn't like I'm some kind
of bonded duckling, downy fluff
toddling after you
all lopsided and starry-eyed

but you sexted me on Shabbat
and now you've traveled 679 miles
back home
leaving me wrapped in my musky sheets
my hand stroking my damp cunt
my nose seeking you in these ruins
remembering your smell.

Your Bones

Your bones are delicate, pointed
nimble, they fly into the air
joyous, lighter than feathers
sharp as your tongue
bitter like a fairy tale from an icy country
I huddle, picking them up excitedly and tossing
throwing your thin white bones skywards
they rest tipsy in the clouds
tilting through the ether
before tumbling scattered to my feet
your bones, a fortune teller's tiny trick.